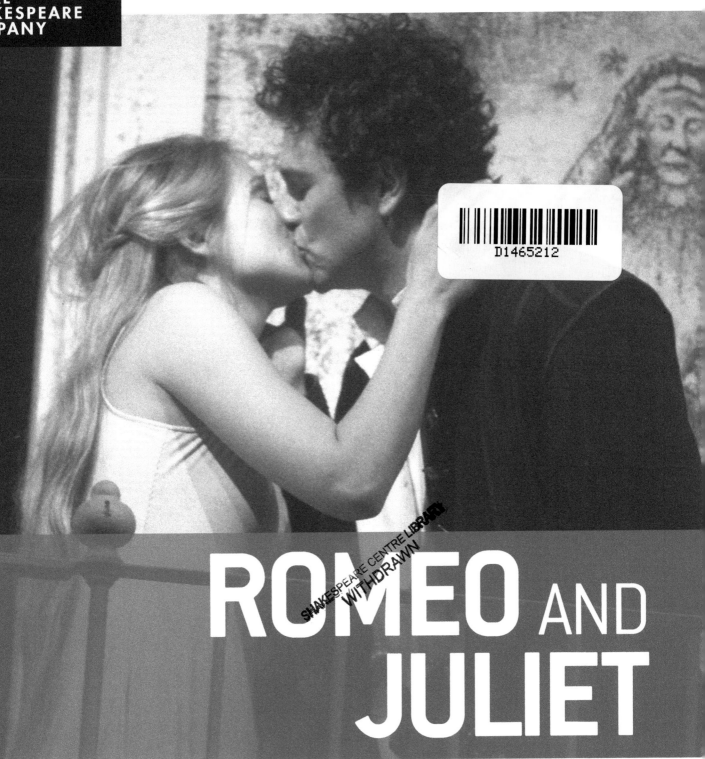

ROMEO AND JULIET

TEACHER GUIDE

OXFORD
UNIVERSITY PRESS

Great Clarendon Street, Oxford, OX2 6DP, United Kingdom

Oxford University Press is a department of the University of Oxford.

It furthers the University's objective of excellence in research, scholarship, and education by publishing worldwide. Oxford is a registered trade mark of Oxford University Press in the UK and in certain other countries

Text © Royal Shakespeare Company 2016

The moral rights of the authors have been asserted

First published in 2016

British Library Cataloguing in Publication Data

Data available

ISBN 978-019-836929-5

10 9 8 7 6 5 4 3 2 1

Printed in Great Britain by Ashford Print and Publishing Services, Gosport

Acknowledgements

Cover and performance images © Royal Shakespeare Company 2016

Cover photograph by Peter Coombs. Other Romeo and Juliet performance images by Ellie Kurttz.

Contents

Romeo and Juliet, *Romeo and Juliet*, 2008

Editing choices

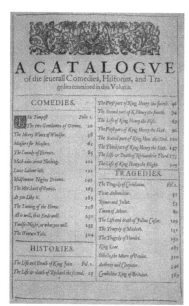

A list of the plays contained in the First Folio of William Shakespeare 1623

Following his death in 1616, two of Shakespeare's friends and colleagues, John Heminges and Henry Condell, put together a collection of his plays which was published in 1623, known as the First Folio, and this edition of the play is based on the First Folio text.

Punctuation

Our text has been edited for punctuation, and choices based on clarity have been made where wording and lineation vary between Folio and Quarto★. Fashions in punctuation change but its purpose is always to support the reader's understanding. In this edition, our motive has been to keep the punctuation as simple and clear as possible but to avoid influencing students' choices. Exclamation marks, for example, are rarely used in the First Folio whereas today's fashion is to use them more liberally. In this edition, they have been used only when they appear in the First Folio or when it is clear an exclamation is required, such as calling out a greeting. In most cases, sentences end in full stops, allowing the students to decide the tone of a line and whether they feel it should be spoken as an exclamation, a statement or a question.

Stage directions

Similarly, there are very few stage directions in the First Folio but those that do exist most probably reflect the stage business as originally performed. Where these stage directions do exist, we have kept them so that students can choose to follow them or not. Generally, Shakespeare gives us important stage directions in the text; for example entrances are often marked by 'Here comes…'. Students are encouraged in the activities to discover directions for action written in the text and to add their own choices about actions and movements appropriate for the scene.

★ The Quarto was a smaller format of publication. As with the larger Folio editions, many versions of the Quarto were produced with variations in editorial decisions.

The apothecary, *Romeo and Juliet*, 2004

Working collaboratively

When a new group of actors and their director come together to rehearse at the RSC, time is spent on the practical, playful process of building a company. This is partly achieved by 'warming up' through a series of physical and vocal games and exercises, before exploring together whichever scenes and speeches are in the rehearsal schedule for that day.

Starter activities

In the classroom, the equivalent to the 'warm up' would be the 'starter' activity, which scaffolds the main activity of the lesson. In a rehearsal-based classroom, starter activities should build physical and vocal confidence, communication skills and positive relationships, as well as introducing any new knowledge required for the lesson. For example, if you are going to ask your students to work in pairs to explore a dialogue, you might start the lesson with a game. If the dialogue you are going to be exploring is full of conflict, the game you choose might be one in which your students can score points against their partner. Or, if you want the focus to be on the quality of the relationship between the two characters, you might ask pairs to make a freeze-frame which shows their initial interpretation of that relationship, before going on to explore the dialogue in more detail.

Grouping

We have left grouping as open as possible, so that you can use the activities flexibly. While some of them can be done as individuals, we recommend that you enable your students to collaborate wherever possible. Interpretation in rehearsal always comes from sharing and valuing each other's ideas, questioning assumptions and speculating possibilities, which we can only do with others. Often the number of characters in a scene will lead naturally to grouping in your classroom. If a scene has four characters, a group of four should explore it. If you don't have the right number of students to make equal sized groups, there is a benefit in having an 'extra' group member who can either bring in another point of view as a non-speaking character (for example, as a servant in a court scene) or fulfil a directorial function, acting as an outside eye for the rest of their group as they decide how to interpret a scene together.

> **Examples of flexible grouping activities include:**
> - Activity 4, page 64
> - Activity 4, page 108
> - Activity 2, page 130

Mercutio and Tybalt, *Romeo and Juliet*, 2004

Questioning

Good questioning is crucial both in encouraging students to experiment with ideas and in leading their reflections after each activity. Students will often have found an embodied understanding through the activities, but without time spent articulating that understanding it can easily dissipate.

Using open questions

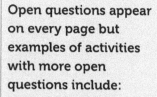

Open questions appear on every page but examples of activities with more open questions include:
- Activity 8, page 92
- Activity 4, page 34

Open questions are often defined as questions to which you cannot respond with one 'right' answer or with a simple yes or no. The questions we offer in these activities are framed to avoid yes/no answers and encourage students to reflect more deeply on the understanding they have gained actively. These questions are far from exhaustive and we would urge you to ask others.

Making personal connections

One successful approach is to ask questions that encourage students to link the emotions and situations of the play with emotions and situations they can relate to from their own experiences and imaginations. Opening questions you can always ask are:

- How did that exercise make you feel?
- What discoveries did you make by speaking the text in that way?

Some students need more time to think and process their thoughts than others. Paired or group reflections are very useful in giving each student more opportunity to express and develop their responses in dialogue with each other. This can be followed by a whole class plenary in which more students can be encouraged to take part because they have had time to formulate their ideas.

Many teachers have found that asking students to record their thoughts and ideas in journals as they work through their study of the play is hugely beneficial and provides personalised notes to return to when completing assessments.

Juliet and the Nurse, *Romeo and Juliet*, 2004

Creating a character

Character motivation

In order for an actor to play a character, they must first understand what motivates their character. The questions that actors and their director ask about the characters in a scene are often deceptively simple: 'Who are they?', 'In what time period and time of day is the scene taking place?', 'Where are they?', 'What are they doing?', 'What are they trying to achieve?', 'Why are they doing that?' It is through these basic questions that the company begin to bring the play to life. By asking these questions of themselves and each other, the company have to search for clues in the text which help them to decide what is motivating the characters.

Developing the 'given circumstances'

Actors pay attention to the 'given circumstances' of a scene, or those things that we know from the text. For example, in asking 'Where are they?', the company might know from the text that a scene is set in 'a room in the castle', but which room? What are the values, social customs and atmosphere of the place? In asking 'Who are they?', the company might know that the characters are father and daughter, but they must work out what the exact nature of the relationship is and how it evolves, the shifting status of the characters, their 'backstory' (or what has happened between them before the play starts), and what has happened in the play thus far to affect the characters and their actions. Character motivation is discovered by actively exploring the evidence in the text to make informed interpretations.

The activities in this resource are designed to help students answer the basic questions about character for themselves: Who? What? Where? When? Why? so that they can work out character motivation. A company of actors rehearsing a play at the RSC ask each other questions all the time, and we recommend that you encourage students to ask each other these questions as they work. Using the activities will offer your students plenty of opportunities to do just that.

Examples of activities requiring students to ask questions about characters include:

- Activity 3 page 84
- Activity 3 page 118
- Activity 1 page 202

Friar Laurence, *Romeo and Juliet*, 2004

Layering

In rehearsal, actors and their director explore the same part of the text in different ways, with the aim of developing a deep understanding of that part of the action. It is a cumulative, layered process, in which multiple possibilities for interpretation are explored. Then, the company make mutually agreed, informed interpretive choices based on the evidence in the text.

Extending learning opportunities

Examples of transferable activities in the opening scenes include:

- Activity 6, page 24 (the speaking activities)
- Activity 7, page 26 (the movement activity)
- Activity 11, page 34 (the reflection activity)

In order to emulate this rehearsal process in the classroom, we recommend offering a series of short activities, which build on each other but explore a different aspect of the text each time. This can enable close reading and active engagement, but avoid students getting bored working on the same part of the text. In this resource, we have usually offered a single activity for exploring the text on each page, for the sake of clarity. But, as you work through the activities with your class, you will notice strategies which could easily be transferred to use with a different part of the text. If there is a particular scene which you want your students to focus on more fully, we hope you will consider transferring some of the activities from other pages to enable a deeper understanding of your focus scene. In this way, we can layer and extend the learning opportunities for our students.

Repeating activities

Examples of activities highlighting structure include:

- Activity 2, page 96
- Activity 3, page 98
- Activity 4, page 148
- Activity 1, page 152

In the rehearsal room, it is common practice for the company to explore each new scene or speech in a play using familiar activities. A shared set of approaches is deliberately developed. Because the strategies are applied to different parts of the text, they feel fresh each time. Similarly, in the rehearsal-based classroom, we deliberately apply the same strategies to different parts of the text so that our students have the opportunity to become familiar and more confident with those activities. In so doing, we build layers of understanding and engagement. As you explore this resource, you will notice strategies that are repeated. We hope you will also notice how the same activities can produce widely differentiated outcomes, simply because they are applied to a different part of the text.

One of the outcomes of using this layered approach can be to highlight the structure of a play. In the many plays where Shakespeare offers a parallel or 'sub' plot alongside the main action, using the same active strategies to explore parallel events in the play can enable our students to see the similarities (and differences) between them.

Creative constraints

In order to test the relationships between characters in an RSC rehearsal room, actors often find it useful to try exercises that put some kind of limitation on how they respond. By applying this limitation, actors make discoveries about what the lines could mean and about their relationship with other characters. Using the same exercises, students can experiment with different ways to interpret a scene and can discuss what feels right for them in expressing the relationship between their characters and why.

Movement choices

In some activities students are asked to choose between simple movements. Giving students simple but specific choices to make removes the fear of 'acting' but also means they can't just stand still and speak because standing still becomes a choice, not a default. In making these simple choices, students find intuitive responses led by the words their own character speaks or the words that are spoken to them. These exercises are also useful for thinking about characters present in a scene who have no, or few, lines. These characters are still required to make the choices about movement and other characters have to respond to what they do.

Examples of activities exploring movement choices include:
- Activity 3, page 48
- Activity 1, page 52
- Activity 6, page 90
- Activity 2, page 144

Speaking choices

In other activities, students are given constraints about how they speak. For example, they can compare how whispering lines and then speaking them loudly brings out different qualities of expression; how reading aloud and swapping reader on each punctuation mark can clarify sense but also express whether a character is feeling calm or agitated; how speaking to achieve a simple objective, like getting another character to look at you, brings language alive by giving a character a reason to speak.

Examples of activities exploring speaking choices include:
- Activity 6, page 24
- Activity 4, page 42
- Activity 1, page 232

Romeo and Juliet, *Romeo and Juliet*, 2010

Speaking text aloud

Unlike many of the other texts we tackle with our students, a play text is intended to be shared aloud, between characters on stage and with the audience. The text is not simply black marks on a piece of paper, but words that are meant to be expressed and received orally and aurally. In the RSC rehearsal room, the company of actors and their director use the text as a script, to be shared. One of the challenges of working with a play which is four hundred years old is that it has been done many times before. Nevertheless, each new company which tackles the play will go through the process of speaking and listening to the words, negotiating meaning until a unique, new version of the play is discovered. We can offer the same opportunity to our students, in a speaking and listening process which can lead to highly engaged and personalised responses to the text.

Making meaning

> **Examples of activities making meaning include:**
> - Activity 8, page 28
> - Activity 2, page 82
> - Activity 3, page 214

A word on the page may appear to have a fixed meaning, but when that word is spoken, the meaning of the word is dependent on the intention of the speaker. Consider for a moment the word 'yes'. We all know the dictionary definition of that word. However, when the word 'yes' is spoken as if the speaker is doubtful, it means something entirely different than when the same word, 'yes', is spoken as if the speaker is excited. Tone, pitch, volume and pace are essential to the meaning of the spoken word. So, in rehearsal, meaning is negotiated by speaking the text aloud, exploring and experimenting until a consensus is reached. The activities in this resource offer students the opportunity to follow the same process.

Getting the language 'in the body'

> **Examples of getting the language 'in the body' include:**
> - Activity 2, page 46
> - Activity 3, page 56
> - Activity 1, page 142

Actors and directors at the RSC refer to 'getting the language in the body', by which they mean doing exercises which connect them with the sound and rhythm of the words. The phonic and poetic quality of the language is as important as the literal meaning of the words. Sound and rhythm are deeply affective, experienced on an instinctive level. By voicing and hearing the words, actors can experience the effect of the language. We can offer the same opportunity to our students by encouraging them to speak and listen to the words through the activities in this resource.

Embodying text

Embodying the text is an actor's job. A fundamental aspect of exploring the plays as plays is being on your feet, stepping into the shoes of the characters, experiencing what it is like to be Beatrice or Juliet, Shylock or Banquo, and able to express your thoughts and feelings as articulately as they do. Working with play texts provides excellent opportunities for developing every student's inbuilt facility for communication skills. Just as most of us naturally and easily learn to speak as very young children, we naturally and easily learn to read body language. Students with English as an Additional Language (EAL) and less confident readers often thrive with this work because they can use their understanding of gesture and tone.

> **Examples of activities exploring body language include:**
> - Activity 2, page 20
> - Activity 3 page 106
> - Activity 6 page 242

Freeze-frames

Freeze-frames are frequently suggested in our activities because they can quickly tap into the key themes in the plays or physically summarise a relationship. For example, a freeze-frame of 'a royal leader and his subjects' created by the students themselves enables a kinaesthetic, imaginative understanding of abstract notions like status and hierarchy to deconstruct through questioning. Freeze-frames of 'brothers' or 'father and daughter' can provide a spectrum of attitudes: love, happiness, fear, disappointment, resentment. Acknowledging these different possibilities can provide a quick and easy insight into the complexity of family relationships. Discussion of these images can lead us into the world of the play by making it relevant to our own worlds. Asking students to create a freeze-frame from a line of text, or asking students to adjust a freeze-frame to reflect or include a line of text are ways to deepen connections between our physical, emotional and intellectual understanding of the text.

> **Examples of activities using freeze-frames include:**
> - Activity 7, page 26
> - Activity 3, page 40
> - Activity 5, page 160
> - Activity 4, page 194

Gestures

Other activities ask students to find 'gestures' for key words. In a similar way to working with freeze-frames, these activities support an intellectual understanding of the text through physical associations. For example, creating gestures for the rich imagery of the oppositional elements in antithesis can support appreciation of the internal conflicts a character feels.

Rhythm

Working with the rhythms of the text can give an actor important understanding of how a character might be feeling. You will notice that activities ask students to engage physically with rhythm through galloping, clapping or tapping. This physical approach makes it very clear when there are variations or disturbances to the rhythm so that students can consider what the variations might suggest about a character's state of mind, and how Shakespeare crafts his writing around unfolding rhythms.

> **Examples of activities exploring rhythm include:**
> - Activity 2, page 54
> - Activity 5, page 66
> - Activity 8, page 180
> - Activity 3, page 236

Glossary

Adjective a word that describes a noun, e.g. blue, happy, big

Anachronism something wrongly placed in the time period represented

Antithesis bringing two opposing concepts or ideas together, e.g. hot and cold, love and hate, loud and quiet

Aside when a character addresses a remark to the audience that other characters on the stage do not hear

Atmosphere the mood created by staging choices

Banter playful dialogue where the speakers verbally score points off each other

Blank verse verse lines that do not rhyme

Body language how we communicate feelings to each other using our bodies (including facial expressions) rather than words

Casting deciding which actors should play which roles

Choreograph create a sequence of moves

Clown an actor skilled in comedy and improvisation who could often sing and dance as well

Dialogue a discussion between two or more people

Dramatic climax the most intense or important point in the action of a play

Dramatic irony when the audience knows something that some characters in the play do not

Emphasis stress given to words when speaking

Extended metaphor describing something by comparing it to something else over several lines

Falling action the part of a play, before the very end, in which the consequences of the dramatic climax become clear

Feeding the lines reading lines aloud a few words at a time so that the actor can repeat them without holding a script

Freeze-frame a physical, still image created by people to represent an object, place, person or feeling

Gesture a movement, often using the hands or head, to express a feeling or idea

Iambic pentameter the rhythm Shakespeare uses to write his plays. Each line in this rhythm contains approximately ten syllables. 'Iambic' means putting the stress on the second syllable of each beat. 'Pentameter' means five beats with two syllables in each beat

Imagery visually descriptive language

Improvise make up in the moment

Irony saying the opposite of what you mean

Monologue a long speech in which a character expresses their thoughts. Other characters may be present

Objective what a character wants to get or achieve in a scene

Obstacle what is in the way of a character getting what they want

Paraphrase put a line or section of text into your own words

Personification giving an object or concept human qualities

Plot the events of a story

Prompt book a copy of the script kept by the stage management team with space for notes and sketches about staging

Pun a play on words

Quatrain a stanza of four lines

Repetition saying the same thing again

Rhyme scheme the pattern of rhymes at the end of lines of a poem or verse

Rhyming couplet two lines of verse where the last words of each line rhyme

Shared lines lines of iambic pentameter shared between characters. This implies a closeness between them in some way

Soliloquy a speech in which a character is alone on stage and expresses their thoughts and feelings aloud to the audience

Sonnet a poem with 14 lines. Shakespearean sonnets are written in iambic pentameter and include three quatrains and a rhyming couplet at the end

Statue like a freeze-frame but usually of a single character

Syllable part of a word that is one sound, e.g. 'dignity' has three syllables – 'dig','ni','ty'

Symbol a thing that represents or stands for something else

Tactics the methods a character uses to get what they want

Theme the main ideas explored in a piece of literature, e.g. the themes of love, loyalty, friendship, family and fate might be considered key themes of *Romeo and Juliet*

Tone as in 'tone of voice'; expressing an attitude through how you say something

Verb a 'doing' or action word, such as *jump, shout, listen*

Vowels the letters a, e, i, o, u